I0758560

Copyright © 2022 by Jim Wolfe.

ISBN 978-1-956691-03-0 (softcover)
ISBN 978-1-956691-04-7 (hardcover)
ISBN 978-1-956691-05-4 (ebook)
Library of Congress Control Number: 2022904364

All rights reserved. No part of this book may be reproduced or transmitted in any form or by any means, electronic or mechanical, including photocopying, recording, or by any information storage and retrieval system without express written permission from the author, except in the case of brief quotations embodied in critical reviews and certain other noncommercial uses permitted by copyright law.

This book is a work of fiction. Names, characters, places, and incidents are the product of the author's imagination or are used fictitiously. Any resemblance to actual locales, events, or persons, living or dead, is purely coincidental.

Printed in the United States of America.

Orion Press
www.orionpressbooks.com
1382 Belmont Road, Raymond, WA 98577

The Art of Hope

of

That We Might Find a Way

JIM WOLFE

Dedicated to the human beings on this Earth, that
they might find a way to peace, love and joy.

And to my dear wife Ginger, my love and inspiration.

CHAPTER 1

The Despair of Hope

She was staring down at the churning waves far below her. It was dark, cold and raining in San Francisco, and Hope was standing in the middle of the vast span of the Golden Gate Bridge, soaked through with a wetness and a miserable chill that seemed akin to the freezing despair she was feeling. The storm had whipped the bay waters far below her into a froth, white and visible even in the dark night without a moon; she could hear the waves churning, as if in a giant washing machine. She had climbed up to stand on one of the huge cables that supported the roadway and was holding onto one of the horizontal cables that served as a handrail. She stood there feeling nothing but despair (as she thought), with that horrible sense that she, personally, had been a failure. So powerful was the wind that the immense steel structure was trembling, creaking, groaning and swaying. A storm warning had been issued, and the authorities had ordered the bridge closed to all traffic for the duration of the storm, and they had set out the barricades, and Hope was totally alone on this huge steel structure, cold, wet and frozen stiff. So thick was the fog and rain that no one, not even the guards watching the security cameras, had observed her as she slipped past the barricades. The low shreds of fog went whipping by, flying in the wind.

She had condemned herself in her own mind, feeling the guilt and remorse for all her all-too-human frailties, failures and misdeeds, great and small. She resolved in her own mind to jump. She gazed down at the churning waves, and then she closed her eyes and whispered, "I have failed. It's over."

"Well, girl, before you go, there's something I want to show you," said a voice from behind her. And even through her eyes remained shut, in her mind's eye she began to see a glimmer of light. She turned around and her eyes were opened, and she saw, standing below her on the roadway, what appeared to be a grizzled old man of about 60 years, and he was saying, "You can jump if you decide to, but first I just want you to look at what I've got here." In his hands he was holding a large rectangular object wrapped in cloth, and it seemed to give off a soft white radiance of its own against the blackness of the storm. He said, "Come down off of there and let's just talk a while."

She suddenly got a death-grip on the handrail, as if she felt once again the pull of her life force. Cautiously she turned around in the howling wind and stood there trembling for a while, afraid to move lest the blast blow her right off the bridge and into the bay. The old man stood silent and patient, as if he knew that she would climb down in perfect safety. And climb down, she did. Slowly she got down and cautiously shuffled over to where the old man was standing.

"Who are you, and what are you doing out here?" she asked.

The old man threw back his head and laughed and replied, "Why, girl, I might ask you the same thing. Just exactly who are you, and what are you doing out here in this beastly weather, thinking about dying when you could be safe at home, drinking hot chocolate by the fire?"

"You don't understand what I've been going through."

"Well, that's seems obvious, don't it? To some folks, what you're thinking of doing out here would seem mighty hard to comprehend. But then again, you might try me — maybe I'd understand some things that you don't."

"I just can't see that."

"Well, that's true. You can't see it. Not yet anyway."

"Who did you say you are?"

"I didn't, but you can just call me Jesse."

She looked and pointed at the large rectangular object he was holding and said, "What have you got there?"

"Oh, this?" he replied carelessly. He held up the object and said, "It's not much, just a little something I brought along because I thought you might find it interesting. I understand that you're interested in art?"

"Why, yes. All my life. How did you know?"

"Maybe someday I'll tell you. Not important right now. For now, I just want you to have a look at this." And the old man pulled off the cloth wrappings and they flew away in the wind. He held up the object for her to see, and she gasped in amazement and disbelief. It was a portrait such as she had never seen before.

"Who…who is that person in the picture?" She asked.

"You don't recognize her?" replied the old man. "Look closer."

The portrait was of a woman such as herself, but more beautiful than ever she could have imagined. Whether she was young or old, Hope could not say. She seemed in the bloom of youth, and yet the lines in her face held the wisdom of centuries. The figure in the portrait seemed made of gold and silver, almost blinding in its brightness, and it seemed alive, moving. It shone with the light of Heaven, the face beamed with joy, the smile dazzled, the eyes danced with an effusive good humor and love.

"No, I don't know her," she replied.

Old Jesse gave a start and looked askance at her, then at the portrait, and back at her again, and he said, "Really? 'Cause believe it or not, I think the person in this picture looks an awful lot like you."

"How could that be? She's so beautiful, perfect, happy. I'm disgusting, a miserable failure. You don't know me, the shame that I feel."

"No, you see, that's where you're wrong: I *do* know, I really do. You're no different than millions of other people on this planet. I've seen 'em all. I've seen the despair. I've seen the darkness in the minds and hearts of people just like you. I've seen the evil it can do. But I'm here to tell you that the way you've seen yourself all these years, that's not the real you. You look inside yourself, and right now you all you see is sin and pain and guilt and shame and sorrow. But I'm telling you that the woman in this portrait, well, that's what the real you looks like, that's how the Creator sees you. Because the Lord Himself painted this portrait of you. This is how He painted you in the Beginning, long before you were born.

"Now, I want you to just think about that for a moment: This painting is the exact image of God that He intended for you, this is His blueprint for you. If you can believe that, then you'll never climb up on this or any other bridge again."

She stood staring for a long while, first at the picture, and then at the old man. She said, "I *want* to believe that. I've *always* wanted to believe that, but I never dared."

"Wanting to believe ain't the same as believing, but it's a place to start. And as far as daring to believe goes, well, look at it this way: It must have taken some daring, some courage, for you to climb up on this bridge, and even more to climb down again — so we'll begin with that, too."

She began to tremble all over in shock. She felt the enormity of what she had almost done enveloping her. She felt sick, she fell to her knees, her face grimaced in grief, she sobbed, and tears began to stream down her face, releasing a flood of pent-up emotion.

The old man knelt by her and placed a hand on her heaving shoulder and said quietly, "It's all right. It's going to be all right now. You did good."

She sobbed, "I, I don't feel like I did good."

"That's OK, too. Just you feel what you feel. You've got a lot of work to do, but you've done plenty of work for one night."

"Will I see you again?" she asked.

"Maybe," He replied, and he stood up and waved his arm and said, "Now, get out of here, shoo! Go on home and have a cup of hot chocolate by the fire." He looked after her as she turned for home and walked away. Then he shouted over the roar of the storm, "Hey, girl! You keep on bein' brave, y'hear? Maybe I'll see you again sometime!"

Hope had turned for home, and then she stopped at the cry of his voice. She looked back, but Jesse was gone, and she felt as if she had awakened from a dream. She was alone on the bridge, with the wind roaring and the fog flying by and the cold rain spattering on the roadway; and yet she felt peaceful and warm inside. The cold rain seemed to wash away the burden of troubling thoughts from her mind; they seemed to be washed from her head all the way down to her fingertips, thence they fell away to the pavement, and she felt her step lightening and quickening. Her head was gradually clearing as she walked for miles through the storm back to her house. She unlocked her door and went inside and shut the door on the storm behind her. Switching on the light, she realized that she had never appreciated how warm and bright and inviting was her own home. She shed her wet clothes and they dropped to the floor, and then she went to her closet and put on her best robe, dry and warm. She had never used her fireplace, and now she wondered why she did not. And so tonight, for the first time she lit a fire in the grate, and then went to the kitchen and prepared herself a steaming mug of hot chocolate; then she returned to the den. The fire was burning bright and hot by then, and she pulled up her chair to the fireside and sipped her drink and watched the dancing flames and smelled the faint aroma of the wood smoke and listened to the crackling and snapping of the burning wood, while outside the wind howled and the rain spattered against the windows, and somehow, for the first time in years, she *knew* that life was good. She was still hurting inside, but then she thought about the woman she had seen in that painting (*could that be the real I?* she wondered), and what the old man had said about her, and it gave her hope. It was all right because she now felt a new strength within her. She drained the last of her hot chocolate and went to bed and slept a sleep of peace as she had never known before. Tomorrow would be the New Day.

CHAPTER 2

The New Day

Hope awoke the next day feeling refreshed, although she still felt that certain pain within her, as though she still could not believe that she was that woman in the portrait. In the grate there were still a few glowing coals left over from the fire of the night before, and so she stoked the fireplace with a few more logs until a good blaze was going again. She walked to the kitchen and fixed herself a cup of coffee and returned to the fireside and engaged in a reverie such as she had never experienced before. She thought about what the Old Man had said about her, the interest in art that she had always had but never really followed in all the years of her life.

But what to do? She had not the most rudimentary training in art, and yet she was aspiring to create art such as humankind had never done before! How was it possible? But then a plan began to evolve in her mind.

Every day for a month, she went down to the San Francisco Museum of Modern Art and perused and studied the paintings and sculptures displayed there, and took notes on every work displayed there, and every artist, and every technique. But most of all, she examined the *effect* of every work, its emotional and intellectual and spiritual impact; she analyzed the *way* in which the artist had managed to achieve the effect, the way it made her *feel*. Eventually, she narrowed her search down to one artist, a certain Monsieur Antoine Aubert, a man of about thirty years, who had emigrated from France to the States some ten years earlier. He had established a studio in San Francisco. She investigated and found that he only instructed the best artists of the best, some of whom had also displayed their works in the same museum.

It was impossible, but she decided to visit Monsieur Aubert's studio anyway, and to try to enlist his assistance in her quest for portraits of the human — and of the divine.

CHAPTER 3

The Instructor

"I am afraid you'll think my story ridiculous," Hope was saying. She had somehow managed to schedule a brief appointment with the famous and accomplished artist, Monsieur Aubert, and was now seated in his studio, cluttered and crammed with works of art.

"Mademoiselle, try me," replied Aubert. "I assure you that I have probably heard stories that sounded more ridiculous."

And so, Hope told her fantastic story of her night on the bridge, of her despair and her climbing up on the bridge, the appearance of the old man, her climbing down again, his revealing of the dazzling portrait, the proclamation that the picture was how she appeared to

God in reality, her breaking down in grief, the old man's consolation, the way she walked home in peace.

While she was relating this story, the instructor seemed completely distracted, and he kept looking away as if uncomfortable and wanting to escape from his situation, trying not to listen. After she had finished, he sat there in silence for some minutes, not wishing to accept the gravity and importance of her experience. Finally, he said in an offhand way, "Well, Mademoiselle Hope, that is indeed a fantastic tale. I only wish that I had the talent to paint a portrait such as you describe. But if as you say your portrait was painted by the Creator Himself, then it must be quite a hopeless task for any mortal to undertake. Yes, quite impossible. I am sorry, Mademoiselle, but what you ask is impossible. I have seen too much of the world to think that this is idea of yours could be the least bit realistic."

She began to protest, but he said, "*Non, cherie,* what you are asking, *c'est impossible!* I am a busy man; I have no time for anyone who is not already an accomplished artist. I instruct only the best of the best in this studio. Think of what you're asking — you, who have had no training in art whatsoever! You would be starting from the very beginning. My time is valuable — do you think you could even afford to pay for my private lessons? Also, I refuse to waste your time. I think perhaps that your time would be better spent if you were to stick with what you *can* do, not what you *cannot* do."

While Aubert was spouting this tirade, Hope remained silent, looking down at her lap with tears starting in her eyes. But then she raised her head, her eyes still streaming, and she looked him straight in the eye, and said in a thick voice, "Monsieur Aubert, you seem to me an upright person, considerate of others, and brutally honest. I value those traits in a person. I appreciate the fact that you refuse to waste others' time and resources, as you would not have them waste yours. Therefore, let me be equally frank with you." She pointed to a canvas in the corner of the room. "You see that painting over there in the corner? It's not bad, but the brushstrokes seem to me a bit stiff and frigid, I see a passion longing to burst out free and unencumbered; and yet it is constrained. Not only that, but the colors aren't quite right: Where there's green, I think a blue shade might have been used to greater effect."

Aubert bristled, and said, "Oh, that is what you think, do you? So now, you're an art critic, *êtes-vous*? And just who do you think created that painting?"

"I haven't any idea."

"*I* painted it. And I tell you that you have not the talent — not to create art, nor to criticize it. And now, Mademoiselle Hope, I beg that you will leave."

She blew past the receptionist, Angelica McKinley, who was throwing a snobbish smile — no, more like a sneer — in her direction. She burst out through the door and pounded along the pavement, with eyes still streaming wet, yet with a jaw set like iron and a face screwed up in fury. Pedestrians and motorists alike gave her a wide berth, as if she might blow them away with one look. Hope hated the man (and his receptionist Ms. McKinley!), and yet at the same time, she reproached herself: She could not believe she had the audacity to criticize someone whose accomplishments were so obviously far above her own. She thought to herself: *Well, now you've done it! You just offended one of the premier art instructors in the world. Good luck now, getting instruction from so much as a first-grade art teacher, or anyone else!*

But she *had* shown the audacity. Where on Earth had *that* come from? It was as if the words had been put into her mouth. But whose words, and from where?

The next day, Hope phoned Monsieur Aubert's studio, but Ms. Angelica McKinley, the receptionist, recognized her voice instantly and told her that Monsieur Aubert was out of town and that she did not know when he would be back. And she got the same result the next day, and the next day and the next. Finally she resolved to just camp out on the sidewalk by the studio, but Angelica had been watching out through the front window and instantly recognized her: She walked out to meet her; and she said, with a scowl and with a voice like ice, that she regretted that Monsieur Aubert was still away from the studio, and that she feared that it was cold outside, and she felt that Mademoiselle Hope would perhaps be much more comfortable at home. This even though as Hope was being lectured thus, Monsieur Aubert himself slipped just behind them and through the studio door.

There was nothing for it but to go home, thought Hope. It *was* cold that evening, and so she got the fire going in the grate, and fixed herself a cup of coffee, and she sat in her chair and just mulled things over. And then, she realized that she had one more trick up her sleeve. When she had been inside the studio, she had noticed that certain of Monsieur's paintings were of destitute, homeless people, the same people as could be found on the sidewalk, right outside his studio. And yet these portraits portrayed a dignity of human beings, regardless of their position in life. And so, it seemed to her that this great artist — this vain, self-centered, conceited man — had revealed a tender, selfless, and compassionate side, and that it might be used to good advantage. For you see, when she had been in high school, she had performed in a few well-received plays, and she had proved an actor of no small talent in the theater. And so now, she dressed herself in ragged clothes, and she dirtied her face with grime, and darkened her teeth, and accentuated the lines around her brow, eyes and mouth, tinted her hair with a hint of gray; and when she had finished with the make-up, she looked indeed like a woman still young, yet haggard, hard-bitten, aged before her time by years of hard living. Looking in her mirror, she practiced thinning and tightening her mouth, furrowing her brow, and narrowing her eyes to display a toughness, a hard, cynical, bitter expression. She put on a large, floppy, beaten hat that concealed part of her face, and that completed the disguise. Then out she went and headed for Aubert's art studio. On the way, a local grocery store lent her — unwittingly —a shopping cart from the parking lot when no one was looking, and she filled it with aluminum cans and other junk, and then continued her way. She feigned the limp and the stiffness of someone who had suffered years of exposure, living and sleeping on cold, hard pavement.

She stationed herself on the sidewalk outside the studio so that Monsieur Aubert might notice her, but so good was her disguise that she was confident that no one, not even Aubert's receptionist, the esteemed *Madame Chienne Condescendante*, would recognize her. She fished a cigarette from the pack of Luckies that the grocery store had also "lent" to her, and lit up, and then she looked for all the world like every other homeless person on that street. Except that she wasn't.

All morning she waited, and around 11 o'clock it began to rain. Most of the other street people headed for the nearest overpass for shelter, but she remained where she was. Around lunch time, Monsieur Aubert emerged from his studio, carrying his umbrella. His eyes met hers, and he felt something: He felt that he must paint this person, cold and wet as she was, bitter, tough, and enduring, as he had painted so many others.

He came up to her and said, "Mademoiselle, I do not wish to be impertinent, but would you mind if I painted your portrait?"

She snorted and smirked with a cynical curl of her lip. She took a drag on her Lucky, blew out the smoke, and replied, "Well, that's a first! OK, but what's in it for me?"

"Perhaps I could buy you lunch?"

"A free lunch? Never heard of such a thing." Then she shrugged and crushed out her cigarette, and said, "But OK, why not? I'm hungry, and it won't be the first time I've rented myself out for payment!"

"Please, come into my studio."

Over the next few hours, Aubert worked on Hope's portrait, and as he did so, she glanced around the studio, admiring his works. She thought to herself: *He really has improved since my last visit.* And when he had finished, he invited her to examine her portrait, and she thought: *Remarkable! This man really can show the face of God in a human being.*

The rain had stopped when they emerged from the studio. They walked to a local café and sat down at one of the sidewalk tables. There were other people sitting at tables around them, cultured people, and they all stared and glared at the pair — the one a flashy, celebrated artist, and his companion a dirty, crude, despised vagabond.

Hope lit another cigarette, took a drag and said, "Everyone is staring at us."

"*Alors*, are they? *Bien*, let them stare."

Hope stared back in defiance at the glaring onlookers. She pushed back her chair, and then she smiled as she slowly, deliberately, insolently put her feet up on the table. She flicked the ash from her cigarette, and said to her companion, "This café is a nice place. Aren't you worried that being seen with someone like me will damage your precious reputation?" she mocked.

He smiled a knowing smile and replied, "You try to mock me, Mademoiselle, but I confess that my reputation is perhaps over-inflated. It can stand a little *de*-flating. And as for the people doing the staring, they can — how do you say? — kiss my ass."

Hope snorted and shook her head in feigned disbelief, but her smile betrayed her amusement.

Aubert smiled in return, and then he said, "Mademoiselle, I truly appreciate your sitting for your portrait with me today." He then fell silent for a time, gazing at Hope with a quizzical look, and he said, "And I confess that there is something different about you: I feel as if we have met before."

"Well, maybe it's just your conceit talking. Maybe you think you have some special intuition, some essential quality, some *je ne sais quois*" said Hope, mockingly. "Because you see, Monsieur, you and I *have* met before." And with those words, she crushed out her cigarette and took off her hat. She relaxed her bitter, tight-lipped mouth, looked him in the eye and smiled a mischievous smile. Her disguise seemed to melt away, and she was revealed to him. He was taken aback, as if he were beginning to perceive a revelation.

"Wait, wait! It is *you,* Mademoiselle Hope!" Aubert cried, and he threw back his head and clapped his hands together and laughed, "This was all a ruse! Well done, well done, indeed! *Actuellement,* I do not mind the joke on me — it was well played. I congratulate you, *tres bien!* And perhaps, I deserved it! *Mais, en vérité,* Mademoiselle Hope, you must be a person possessed of exceptional talent, perseverance, and good humor (*and* great daring, I might add!), if you could pull that off! *Bien,* I admit defeat, I surrender, I will take you on as *protégée.*"

But Hope could not help herself taking one more dig at this vain man's ego. She put her hat back on at a rakish angle, and in an instant, she was that cynical vagabond once more, and sneering she said, "It's about fuckin' time!"

He chuckled and shrugged, and said, "*Alors,* perhaps I deserved that, as well, Mademoiselle, but now let us get serious and down to business. *En vérité,* I have not stopped thinking about your visit, and your wish to study art with me in my studio. You must forgive my reaction; I am a prima donna, and therefore an incurably vain man and easily offended. I must also apologize for the rudeness of my receptionist in sneering at you as you were walking out the door. I fear that I have trained her too well in the art of boosting the ego of her employer. I examined that picture all night and thought about your criticism, and I must confess that I can see your point of view. I do not entirely agree with your assessment, but that is beside the point: Few people would have had your degree of insight, and fewer still the courage to be so brutally honest with me, as you put it. Come to my studio tomorrow morning at seven o'clock sharp, and we will begin."

"No, Monsieur Aubert, this must be done in secret. No one can know about this."

He thought a minute, and said, "*Alors*, you are right again. When it comes to matters of destiny, one cannot be too careful. Come at seven tomorrow evening and come to the back entrance."

CHAPTER 4

The Lessons

But Monsieur Aubert did not make the going easy for Hope: On the contrary — he seemed intent on making life as difficult as possible for her. He was unrelenting in his criticism of her work: He attacked it savagely, even going so far as to throw a painting of hers into the fireplace in his studio, or to tear it to pieces in his rage.

Hope felt that his attacks were personal, so that if he attacked her work, he was attacking *her*. Nothing that she did was good enough for him. Every morning, after a long night at the studio, she would stride back to her house, weeping in rage; and yet every evening, she was back again at the studio, hard at work. She felt that it was a contest of wills between her and her instructor, and she gritted her teeth as tears streamed down her cheeks; but she kept painting even as he hurled a barrage of criticism at her at every turn.

And yet, as Monsieur Aubert saw it, it was certainly *not* a contest of wills. No, he saw this as the opportunity of a lifetime, a moment to be seized, a chance to enable this student to surpass every accomplishment he had made in his distinguished career; but he had to keep thrashing, as a jockey uses a riding crop to drive a thoroughbred to surpass every champion that has gone before. He was using his vanity and conceit, even his very reputation, to conceal his true motivation. If she kept thinking that this was a contest of wills, as long as she believed that everything he was doing was being done out of his conceit, then he knew that she would keep fighting out of sheer defiance, he knew that she would never quit. And *alors*, he realized, if she did quit, then it was not meant to be. He would give it all for this one student. Monsieur Aubert knew that if Hope could survive this trial, then she could accomplish anything.

CHAPTER 5

The Gift

One rainy, windy night, Antoine Aubert was working in his studio, when he glanced out the front window and thought he saw Hope, his student as she strode by in a hurry. "*Qu'est-ce que c'est?*" he said to himself, and he grabbed his hat and coat, went out, locked the door and hurried after her at some distance. Yes, it was Hope, and he hurried after her as she strode along on her long, strong legs.

He followed her for some miles, and she seemed to be heading for the Golden Gate Bridge, and he began to realize why, as he remembered her fantastic story about her epiphany there. He watched as she slipped past the barriers, and he did the same. Soon she arrived at the middle of the span and saw her objective: a young woman standing on the giant bundle of cables, preparing to jump. Aubert slipped to one side of the bridge and kept out of sight; he crept forward in the shadows until he was close enough to hear and see what was going on.

Hope was saying to the terrified young woman standing on the brink of eternity, "You know, I've stood right where you're standing now. And while I was standing there someone came up and talked to me. I'm going to tell you just what he told me. He said that it must have taken a lot of courage for me to climb up there, and even more to climb down again. And I did climb down, and now here I am with you."

"I bet you think I'm a coward for thinking of dying."

"No, not a bit. I don't think that at all. See, I think it took a lot of courage for you to climb up there."

"You're just saying that to make me feel better."

"No, I'm not. You see, the way I look at it, you're examining your whole life up to the present moment with no consolations. *No consolations*, mind you: You want to see things just as they are. And there's hope in that. You're wondering if your life 'measures up,' so to speak. They say the unexamined life is not worth living. Takes a lot of courage to review one's life with no consolations, because if you can do that, then you've managed to stare death right in the face.

"I've examined my life and decided it's not worth living."

"I thought that too, once, when I was standing right where you are now.

"What made you climb down again?"

"It was hope. There's an art to creating hope. It comes from your relationships to other people. If you just nurture those relationships, you'll create hope for others. And if you'll create hope for others, you'll find there's hope for yourself. And so, I repeat to you what someone said to me: I think it took a lot of courage for you to climb up there to face death, and it will take a lot more courage for you to climb down again and face life. But believe me, you've got that courage in you, I can see it. And I guarantee that if you climb down, your life will get better, you'll feel better. There'll be a lot of hard work ahead of you, and there'll be a lot of ups and downs; but if you'll just try, you'll find it rewarding. Not only that: If you'll just make the effort, you may find that you're being helped by unseen hands. Trust me: If you'll just come down, you'll feel as if you'd returned from the dead."

Hope paused, and they both stood silent for a while in a certain serenity while the storm raged on. Then Hope said, "I'll tell you what: I'll make you a deal. I'm going to give you a present. No, more than that: I'm going to *make* a present for you right now. I'm going to do a sketch of you. I'm going to show it to you when I'm done. And then you look at that picture, and if you like it, then you climb down, and I'll give you that portrait for free. Is that a deal?"

The young woman's hair hung in lank strands, clinging wetly to her face, her clothes were soaked through, and she was pale and freezing cold and shivering. "You're going to sketch me? Like this? I'm a mess!"

"A little cold and wet can't conceal the real you from me. Trust me."

She shrugged her shoulders in resignation and said, "Well, OK, whatever…"

"Good! It's a deal, then," said Hope, and she took out her waterproof pad and pen, but she didn't draw right away. She stood looking at her subject, taking in the lines of the face, the expression, the pain, the posture of the body. Then, without withdrawing her gaze from her subject, without even glancing at her sketch pad, she began to draw with swift, sure strokes of her pen. Every line was drawn from her unconscious, immediately, without analysis or deliberation. Within five minutes she had finished.

Hope held it up for her subject to see. "Well, what do you think?"

The portrait, though small and made by human hands, still had something of the beauty and the divine power of the visage of Hope drawn by the Almighty.

"It's beautiful. That couldn't be a picture of me, could it?"

"I thought the same thing when I saw my portrait."

"Who? Who showed you your portrait?"

"Oh, some old man. I didn't believe it at first, either. The portrait seemed too perfect, too beautiful."

"The old man, who was he?"

"I don't really know. He was standing right where I am now on this very spot, and then he was gone."

"Will you disappear, like he did?"

Hope laughed at this question, but then she said, "No, I won't disappear."

"I still can't believe that's me."

"But you like the picture, don't you?"

"Like it? I love it!"

"Will you climb down now?"

"But I just *can't*."

Hope laughed and replied, "You've got no choice now — you've got to climb down. We made a deal, remember? If you like the picture, then you come down. A deal's a deal."

And so, the young woman, trembling in every limb with cold and terror, climbed down until she was standing on the roadway.

Hope said, "See, I knew that you had it in you. What's your name?"

"Mine is Sarah. And what's yours?"

"You can call me Hope. And now, Sarah, I give this portrait to you. Oh, and I want you to do one more thing. You look at this portrait every morning, and look at yourself in the mirror, and realize that those two beings are one and the same."

"That's all?"

"Yup, that's all."

Sarah took her picture and walked away. She disappeared into the storm, and at that moment, Aubert stepped out from the shadows. Hope gave a start and gasped, but then she recognized who it was, and said, "Monsieur Aubert, what are you doing here?"

For a moment, Aubert was silent, just gazing at her with a smile of admiration on his face; but then he said, "*Pardon-moi,* Mademoiselle Hope, I did not mean to startle you. You see, I was working late, and I saw you pass by my studio, and something told me that I should follow you. I am glad I did, for I tell you, I have never in my entire life witnessed anything like that. Your work, *c'est magnifique!* Tonight, you have repaid my faith in you, many times over. And now, I must release you from any further lessons in my studio."

Hope was stunned, and she said, "What do you mean, you release me? I have so much more to learn."

"Perhaps, *cherie.* We all have much to learn, *n'est ce pas?* But I am afraid that you will not learn it from me. You are too good for me now. You are now the master. You have proven that much to me tonight. It was a rare privilege to see you at work. Art is a passion, but for me, it remained only an intellectual exercise. I never dreamed that it could be so great a power for good. To give people hope — I wish *I* could do that! *C'est trés, trés bien!*"

"Maybe *I* could teach *you,*" she said with a wry smile.

He smiled in his turn and shook his head and said, "Alas, *non, cherie!* I am afraid that my conceit, my ego, would not permit it," and they both laughed. "And in any case, this destiny is yours, not mine. For me, it is enough that I have helped you to find it."

Hope smiled, and said, "Monsieur Aubert, you *did* give me hope when you admitted me to your studio."

Aubert recalled how severe he had been upon Hope, and he said, "I am afraid that I was terribly hard on you in your lessons. There was no other way. *En conséquent,* I cannot apologize in all honesty."

"Don't be sorry, Monsieur Aubert. The way I see it, I was only being tested."

He smiled and said, "Correct, Mademoiselle Hope, *c'est exactement ça.* I had to make sure of you and your motivation. And I had to make sure *you* were sure. You passed with flying colors."

Hope sighed. Aubert noticed how her shoulders were sagging with emotional exhaustion from her efforts of the evening, and he said, "*Alors, Mademoiselle,* tonight you have worked very hard, and you seem very tired. Please, allow me to walk you home." And together, hand in hand, they walked for miles back to her house, not speaking a word, yet comfortable in their complete companionship. At her door they spontaneously turned and hugged one another warmly. He squeezed her and said softly, "*Bonne nuit, cherie!* Perhaps we shall meet again."

CHAPTER 6

A Career of Hope

And so, Hope embarked on her lifelong career of giving hope to lives that seemed to have none, uplifting the downtrodden, heartening the despairing, making people happy and content with themselves, just as they were, without expectation. In every case, she found that the cause of despair was a false expectation of themselves, usually due to a concern over what others might think of them; and in that concern they lost sight of themselves as beings beautiful in themselves. The ugliness and shame they perceived within themselves was due to the expectations from without. But Hope could manage to reveal their true selves to themselves, just as they were, just as the Creator intended them to be.

But sometimes things did not seem to go so well, as Hope found to her great disappointment and horror. For some people whom she tried to save, truly they had no hope left. More than one person had jumped from the bridge, right in front of her: They seemed to slip right through her fingers at the very moment when she thought they might turn away from death. At those times, though she had become a person of great faith, Hope would feel agony for those victims, she would share their sense of complete despair, she would rail and rage and shake her fists at God, and a sense of complete failure would engulf her, and her fingers would go limp and allow her blank pad and pen to fall to the pavement, and she would drop to her knees and weep — she would feel as if she were going to die of grief. But she did not die, and though at first, she was unaware of it her empathy for those victims was gradually becoming a kind of prayer — a prayer and a hope that those who had chosen to jump might yet be saved. It was a prayer that God would save them, even though — or perhaps especially because — they had condemned themselves. And once again, Hope found hope in faith. She had been gifted with unusual powers and she realized that having those powers was all right; but she also found that she had severe limitations; and yet in time she discovered that having those limitations was all right, too. There existed only One without limitations, she learned, and that One was God, and God alone. And so, she began to perceive that whatever happens, though a person might fail, and though one might suffer and live with pain and sorrow, still *all is well.*

CHAPTER 7

The Despair of the Master

And so, Hope continued to live out her destiny, happily and contentedly. She had not seen her mentor, Monsieur Antoine Aubert, for about five years. However, one evening she felt the familiar feeling come over her, the sense that someone was in danger on The Bridge once again. She put on her raincoat, and gathered up her waterproof pad and pen, and headed out into the storm.

She approached the usual spot in the middle of the giant span, where the huge bundles of supporting cables swung lowest to the roadway, and she suddenly stopped short when she saw a familiar figure standing up there with tousled hair and lined face, but also with bowed head and shoulders.

"Monsieur Aubert is that you?" she cried. "What are you doing out here?"

"Yes, Mademoiselle Hope, it is I."

"Monsieur, this is not possible."

"Cherie, I was hoping that you would come."

"Well, here I am, but I still don't understand what we are doing here."

"I know you will say that I have so much to live for. I have my art and my studio, I am successful, I have more than enough money and plenty of followers. And yet, I am wretched, Mademoiselle Hope, totally wretched."

"We talked about this, you know."

"I thought that perhaps, if you would sketch me, and show me the real me, as you have done for so many people, I could find hope for myself again."

Hope thought for a while, and then she said, "No, Monsieur Aubert, I can't sketch you. Because in truth, your despair is an illusion. I have no doubt that your agony is real, but it is not true despair. It is a mere fabrication. You have less cause for despair than anyone I have helped on this bridge. Since your despair is not real, I cannot give you hope. Even were I to try to sketch the real you, the image would remain lifeless, and you would remain disappointed."

"Then Mademoiselle Hope, what am I to do?"

"Monsieur Aubert, understand this: I have been fortunate enough to help people who have stood where you are standing now; and in every single case, their hope lay in taking a step that required more courage than climbing up to where you are now. It took more even more courage for them to climb down. But I don't think that's where your problem lies.

"Monsieur Aubert, I've heard it said that we human beings live our lives in the stories we create about existence, that we are forever trying to live out a drama of our own creation. And I found that to be true, when I was standing where you are standing now. But trying to live out a story becomes a problem for us, because Reality — which is identical with the Lord God — never conforms to *our* story; therefore, there is always a tension between the story of our lives and Reality. It causes us great suffering, great shame and guilt and frustration and anger; and so, the question becomes: How are we to live in harmony with Reality? How are we to come out of the story and truly live? You see, it may have taken some courage for you to ask for my help, to request me to sketch the real you, as you put it. But in your case, I think that what it will take is for *you* to draw the real you. Now, *that* will take even more courage, and it remains the only thing that has a real chance of working.

"Monsieur Aubert, you see, there is no hope in the pursuit of perfection. The only hope is to see that perfection which is already there. It is within, not without."

"Within us, you mean?" asked Aubert.

"Within us, within all things. You only have to dig beneath the surface to find hope and joy and beauty within.

"Monsieur Aubert, you are the most egotistical man I have ever known, but you might be forgiven for it. Lord knows, *I* have forgiven you for it. But will you forgive *yourself* for it? When will you realize that your conceit, your egotism is not such a terrible thing, but rather a defense — a *God-given* defense that has helped you to cope during your whole life? We all of us should be so humble — yes, *so humble* — as to gratefully accept our defense mechanisms as God-given. And if you can accept that in yourself, then there's a chance that you could accept it in others. Think on human weakness — the weakness that all of humanity shares with you — and be thankful. Consider the compassion that God shows for that weakness. Remember your compassion for those less fortunate than yourself, focus on it, and then create a sketch of yourself. Good night, Monsieur Aubert, and good luck." And Hope turned and walked away.

"Wait! Wait, Mademoiselle Hope!" cried Aubert, but it was too late. She had vanished into the night. Aubert climbed down and stood there on the roadway. He looked about in every direction, but there was no sign of her, except that suddenly he looked down and saw that she had left her waterproof pad and pen lying there, spattered with rain, on the roadway. Hesitantly, he picked them up, and walked back to his studio. He left the lights off, and the workshop remained in near darkness. He placed Hope's sketch pad on an easel, picked up the pen, then sat down on a stool and stared at the pad for some time. Then he closed his eyes and contemplated what Hope had said to him: *Think on your weakness and be thankful. Realize that your conceit is a God-given defense. And if you can accept that weakness in yourself, then there's a chance that you can accept it in others. Remember your compassion for the less fortunate and sketch yourself.*

And Aubert, unconsciously, without even opening his eyes, raised the pen and began to sketch — what, exactly he did not know. The pen seemed to move and draw of its own accord, and yet he was aware of strong, sure, yet delicate, sweeping strokes. His mind lost all sense of time; he had no idea how long he remained at the task; but at last, it was done. The pen seemed to stop, then dropped to his side.

He opened his eyes and was astounded at the result, as Hope's subjects had been astonished at hers. The picture was more like — and unlike — himself than he could have imagined. The features were there — the tousled hair, the proud, lean face, the lines of deep guilt and anger and shame. At first the drawing was painful for him to look at; but then, gradually, it seemed to him that it revealed the dignity and the beauty of a soul that was unique in all the world. For the first time in his life, Monsieur Antoine Aubert, one of the premier artists in the world — this vain and conceited and troubled man — felt humble and content and happy with himself, deeply flawed though he might seem. He suddenly recalled something he had heard or read long before, though he could not recall exactly where: *The Kingdom of Heaven is within you.* Truly, he perceived, that Kingdom was within. If you would find happiness, don't seek perfection without. Look within and find the perfection that is already there. The face of God had been revealed to him in the drawing of himself, as Hope's sketches had shown that same visage to her subjects, and as the old man had shown that face to Hope.

CHAPTER 8

The Critics

"Mademoiselle Hope," said Monsieur Aubert, "there is something that I need to do."

Hope thought to herself, *What now?*

He realized what she must be thinking, and said, "No, please, it is not what you think. It is just that I need a third person, an objective opinion of your work. Would you mind if I showed your paintings to some of my colleagues?

"Are you crazy?" replied Hope. We agreed to keep this a secret."

"*Oui, oui, Mademoiselle, absolument.* I would share your work anonymously, no one will know the true author.

"Well, seems a shame, but if that's the way it has to be, OK. But if you give me away, I'll kick your ass!

And Monsieur Aubert did share her work, with some of the best artists and critics and collectors in the world, and he had a terrible time protecting the identity of his protégée, so powerful was her work. They demanded to know who this discovery was, and they offered to buy her paintings for huge amounts of money — so much money that Monsieur Aubert had to confide in her: "Mademoiselle Hope, we cannot ignore the value of your work! Won't you sell?"

"Don't you get it? This is not about money, it's about something bigger than that, bigger than you or I or anything else in this world!"

"Then, *cherie*, let us give back the gift, to speak. Let us sell but do it in such a way that no one will ever know the identity of the true author."

"What about the sheer amount of money? Won't it arouse suspicion?"

"*Oui, oui*, we must do something to avoid arousing suspicion."

Hope thought for a minute, and then she said, "I've got it. You sell in secret, and accept the money, and you set up a foundation to help the homeless people, the ones I've seen outside your studio, the ones you've painted. I won't accept a cent."

Monsieur Aubert's face turned sad, and he said, "You have seen them, then? You have seen my paintings of those noble, beautiful, destitute people?

Hope laid down her brush and her palette. In a soft voice she said, "*Oui,* Monsieur, I have seen them. And trust me, I would not be here, taking lessons from you, if I had not noticed and admired those paintings on my first visit to your studio. Because you see, Monsieur Aubert, not only had you to judge *me* worthy, but I had to judge *you* worthy."

Monsieur Aubert's face fell, and tears sprang into his eyes, and he cried, "What right have I, what right have I? Those poor people, I paint their portraits, I take them to lunch, I sell their portraits for a fortune while they go back to the streets, trying to eke out a living. I am a petty man. I am ashamed, Mademoiselle Hope, ashamed beyond description."

"But you revealed their dignity, you presented the face of God in your portraits of those poor people. You bore witness to it, and the public will see that face in your portraits. Trust me, that's worth something."

"I am ashamed, so terribly ashamed."

Hope was silent for a while, and then she said, "I understand. Then, Monsieur Aubert, *use* the shame. *Use* the shame for the cause of Good. Because if you will, then you may find yourself being helped by unseen hands. After all, The Way is all about finding the Better Way."

Astonished, he looked up. "Mademoiselle Hope, what do you mean, helped by unseen hands?"

"Only this: That God Himself would be pleased to aid you in your endeavor, if you will but try."

Aubert was silent and thought for a while, and then he looked her in the eye and asked earnestly, "Mademoiselle Hope, how do you do it? How do you find hope in everyone, even in such a spoiled, wretched, conceited man as I?"

"These feelings that we human beings have, all of them, they are all gifts, if we but have the eyes to see it. The shame and the guilt may be painful; therefore, they may seem a punishment; they may even seem God's condemnation of Man, but I swear to you they are not. They are gifts, though you may not realize it yet. And trust me, Monsieur Aubert, though you may feel convinced that you are wretched and conceited, I sincerely doubt that God sees you that way."

CHAPTER 9

A Time of Reckoning

And so, Monsieur Aubert became a new man, and yet remained always the same. He began to see clearly himself, his sins, his transgressions, the lies he had told himself and others, the many defenses he had employed, often putting himself above and ahead of others. At first he wondered why he had done these things, why he had done things that had hurt other people, but as he contemplated and meditated, he began to see that — unjust though he may have been — there were reasons for the things he did: They had enabled him to survive, and therefore they were worth something; and furthermore, he could not have done otherwise because he was only a weak and imperfect human being like everyone else.

He called his friend Hope on the phone the next day and invited her to lunch, and to her he expressed all these thoughts and feelings he had been having. Hope noticed the way he looked her steadily in the eye as he confessed it all: calmly, candidly, sincerely, in the most matter-of-fact manner; and she seemed to sense in him a growing life and peace and joy as he spoke, as if he had discovered a treasure, the lode of precious gold that he had been searching for all his life. His voice, his face, his whole being proclaimed: *All is well!*

And Hope, as she was listening to Monsieur Aubert, smiled and nodded and thought to herself: *This is the <u>real</u> man. The more he sees himself clearly, and the more he confesses and accepts his imperfection, the more perfect he becomes.* She suddenly recalled a portrait she had seen in his studio. At the time, she had not recognized the person in that sketch, but suddenly the revelation struck her that it was Aubert: It was he as he had sketched himself after Hope had abandoned him on the bridge, and she had told him that she could not do his portrait, that he would have to do it himself. And sketch his portrait, he had done. He was becoming himself by letting go, without any attempt at changing himself.

And yet, change he did. He became quieter, less angry and judgmental of other people; and yet he became louder, too, as if he would proclaim his newfound hope and joy to all the world.

Aubert's receptionist, the proud and disdainful Angelica McKinley, who had chased off Hope more than once, was completely taken aback by the changes that were being revealed in him. When she was rude or snobbish to a customer at the front desk, Aubert would at once intervene with an easy and polite manner, and yet he would never rebuke or embarrass her. And once after one of those encounters Aubert was passing outside the women's room in his studio and seemed to hear someone crying in there, and he thought he recognized his receptionist's voice. He knocked softly on the door, and asked, "Mademoiselle McKinley, are you in there?"

There was a startled silence for a moment, and then her voice came back thickly through the door: "Yes, Monsieur Aubert."

"Are you alone? May I come in?"

A muffled sobbing came through the door, and then: "Yes, Monsieur Aubert."

And Aubert slowly opened the door and found Ms. McKinley weeping into her handkerchief, and he thought he could guess the reason, but he gently asked anyway, "Mademoiselle McKinley, what is wrong?"

And she answered, "Monsieur Aubert, I don't know what to do. I have tried to do as you would do, I have tried to maintain the standards of this studio, I have tried to keep away people who might not be worthy of the dignity of this establishment, as you have done." She paused and then she sobbed, "But, but sometimes… sometimes I was mean to them."

Aubert stood there and nodded his head. He felt a pang of guilt, because he felt responsible. Angelica had only done as he would have done. He replied quietly, "And you did those things for me, did you not? Out of a sense of loyalty to me?"

She started, as if she had never consciously considered this fact. A flicker of a smile crossed her face, and she said, "Why, yes, Monsieur Aubert. That's exactly it. But suddenly, you are so kind and considerate of everyone — everyone! And it, it makes me ashamed of the way I have behaved."

"*Ah, non,* Mademoiselle McKinley," said Aubert, laying a hand on her shoulder, "It is all right. If anyone should be ashamed, it is I. I have behaved shamefully, arrogantly, toward many people. Everything you have done while working in this studio, you have done out of consideration for me, and therefore, it is worth something. It is worth a great deal to me."

"And yet, you don't seem ashamed. I have worked so hard to obtain your approval. I have always tried too hard to get approval from others. I think so poorly of myself."

"No, Angelica" — and for the first time, she noted that he had called her by her first name — "perhaps you *have* worked hard to obtain approval from others, but I would not say '*too* hard.' Approval-seeking is not such a terrible thing: It is a defense; it is a way of coping. It has enabled you to survive all your life, and now here you are, working in this studio, and I am glad you are here; therefore, your approval-seeking, too, has been worth something. Even in your approval-seeking, there was something perfect. Perhaps something to be thankful for."

"Monsieur Aubert, how do you do it? How do you suddenly make everything positive?"

"Ah, Mademoiselle Angelica, if you would learn the answer to that question, then I invite you to meet the real master. I am but a poor student."

"A master greater than you, Monsieur? How can that be? Who could it be?"

Aubert smiled, and replied, "Mademoiselle Angelica, I confess it would not be terribly difficult to find someone greater than I. But you shall see. Stay after work tomorrow, and I will introduce you." And with a wry and knowing smile, he added, "I think that you will be astonished, and not disappointed."

And so, she stayed late after work. Monsieur Aubert phoned Hope, and she came late. Hope knocked on the door, and Angelica McKinley was indeed astonished: Here was the same person whom she had shamelessly sneered at and turned away from the studio, several times. Now, almost she felt too embarrassed to unlock the door to let her in, and yet at the same time she was too ashamed to ignore her. She sat at her desk and stared toward the door for a minute, then she fumbled in her desk for her keys. She stumbled to the door and tried to insert a key into the lock, dropped the whole bunch to the floor, recovered them, and unlocked the door. Hope realized the embarrassment Angelica was going through, and she covered her mouth as she laughed and watched these antics through the glass door.

Aubert had noticed Hope's arrival and advanced to the door with hand outstretched, and said, "Ah, Mademoiselle Hope. Let me introduce Mademoiselle McKinley, my receptionist. Angelica, this is Mademoiselle Hope. This is the real master, whom I was telling you about."

Angelica was still trying to recover from her embarrassment, but Hope smiled and extended a hand and said to her, "It's a great pleasure to know you."

Hesitantly, Angelica extended her hand, and she stammered, "Ms. Hope, you and I...we...we have met before...under...unfortunate circumstances."

Hope laughed and squeezed her hand warmly, and replied, "No, not so unfortunate! Let me assure you it is a pleasure to finally know you — under better circumstances!"

"Monsieur Aubert tells me that you are quite the master now."

Hope laughed again and replied, "Well, he keeps saying that, but then again, Monsieur Aubert has become uncommonly kind, don't you think?"

"He does seem so."

"Enough, ladies, enough!" said Aubert. "You are toying with me, and the evening is wasting away. And now down to business! Mademoiselle Hope, if you will assist Mademoiselle McKinley, please. She has been suffering terribly and needs your assistance!

And Hope placed her pad on the easel, and picked up her pen, and began to draw Angelica McKinley's portrait. She drew her true self despite her pettiness, her sneers, and her haughtiness — and yet she did not. She celebrated and honored those very defenses that God had provided, it was if she gave thanks for them, for the very things that had enabled her to survive to the present moment, so that she might be in communion with Aubert and Hope. When she had finished, the resulting image astounded Aubert and Angelica: The layers of pettiness and disdain were still there, and yet so transparent were they that something pure and innocent was shining through them. It was Love, and Aubert was beginning to recognize it for what it was. In fact, he had already begun to recognize it, even as he was talking with her a short time before. All that she had done for him was out of love for him, although (as she thought) it would have been inappropriate for her to express it; therefore, she had been ashamed of it. And because of that shame, she had contrived to try to protect him and his studio with a sneering haughtiness.

But now, all was revealed to Angelica. She had been totally unconscious of her motivation — until now, that is, until Hope had revealed it; and now she was angry with herself and ashamed in front of Aubert and Hope. She wanted to appear perfect in front of her friends; she would have preferred never to reveal what she had concealed for so long. But little did she realize that that was how the forces of Darkness were striving to keep her under their control — through shame and self-hatred. In a panic and a rage, she snatched up the pad that Hope was sketching on, and crumpled it up, and hurled it into the fireplace. She raced toward the door, feeling that she could never face Aubert, or Hope, or anyone again: She flung open the door and ran down the street.

Aubert and Hope glanced at one another and in an instant understood where Angelica was going. They both jumped up and raced for the door; and on the way, something told Hope that she would need a pad and pen, and she grabbed them from a table as together they ran for the door and headed down the street. Turning right on Highway 101 they ran for miles, making for the Golden Gate Bridge.

They were almost to the entrance of the bridge when they saw the dim, lithe form of Angelica sprinting onto the span; but before they could reach her, there appeared what seemed to be an old man, Jesse, the very man that had saved Hope, the man who had shown her the portrait of her true self. He strode in front of Hope and Aubert, out onto the roadway and held up his hands and cried, "Stop, stop! Stay where you are! I know you are friends of Angelica's, but you can't help her now. Leave this to me!" And Hope and Aubert suddenly stopped and stood as stiff as boards, and the old man turned and raced after Angelica, as she disappeared into the fog and the darkness.

The night turned darker, and the storm increased in its fury. Hope felt a fear and a sudden horror for Angelica, and unconsciously her hand sought Aubert's, and he sought hers. Somewhere ahead of them, in the darkness and the storm, a battle was raging for Angelica's very soul. They struggled together, and at last they broke free of the power that seemed to be holding them fast, and together they raced onto the bridge.

They ran onto the middle span, where before, so many lives had hung in the balance, and then once again they stood fast, rooted to the roadway in horror at the sight that met their eyes.

Angelica was standing perilously on top of one of the huge cables, exactly where Hope and so many others had stood, but now it was different. Always before, there was only one person present; but now — and maybe it was only a trick of the fog and the wind and rain in the streetlights — now Angelica seemed to be staring, as if transfixed, at an Entity, leering and dark and huge and hardly to be distinguished from the storm itself, with a face full of malice and hatred. It seemed to be laughing, roaring with a cruel laughter. But that was not how Angelica saw that being. To her, it seemed to be reaching out with sympathy and compassion for her shame and her pain and her suffering, tempting her. To be rid of her suffering, all she had to do was to step off into empty space; but it was all a lie.

Jesse was climbing up to stand beside her, and he was saying, "Angelica, look at me!" And slowly, she turned and averted her gaze from the dark entity and looked at Jesse, who continued, "Don't look at it, Angelica — it's the Enemy."

"The Enemy? What do you mean?

"Just what I said: it's the only Enemy that you really need to fear. He would swallow you up forever and never allow you to escape, if he had his way."

Her eyes fell, and then they seemed to be drawn back to the Darkness again.

"Don't look, Angelica!!"

"But he promises comfort and rest from the shame and agony that I'm feeling!"

"No, Angelica! look at me." And once again she averted her eyes and looked at Jesse, who continued: "He can't promise you anything, Angelica, except to capture you and torment you, if you let him. He's powerless to do anything — except to lie and deceive you. Now let me show you something." And Jesse gently grasped her arm, and carefully he turned her so she could see her friends Hope and Aubert standing below them on the roadway. "You see, Angelica, your friends have followed you here. They could have gone home where they would be safe and warm; but instead, for your sake they chose to come here to be with you, they have foregone all comfort and security. They are risking their lives to help you. I tried to stop them coming here; I even put a restraint on them to keep them safe, but their love for you is too great; they broke free. They love you."

And Aubert called out, "*Oui*, Angelica, we love you, Hope and I, but *I* love you in a special way."

"Listen to him, Angelica!" cried Hope. "Love can save you yet! You must believe me: God is love. You must trust in a God that is love. You have seen the Enemy, but you can't see God — not yet. Have faith in the things that you cannot see! Turn away from Darkness and climb down."

But Angelica did not climb down. She swayed to and fro, unsure of herself, half-striving to be free, yet half-desiring to submit to the Darkness.

On a sudden inspiration, Hope took up her pen and her pad in hand and began to sketch furiously; but she was not sketching Angelica. Finally, when she was finished, Hope climbed up beside Angelica in the roaring storm, and she carried her sketch with her, and she held up that sketch and she shoved it into the very face of the cruel entity facing them; and she cried: "Lucifer! That's your real name, isn't it? Also known as the Enemy, the Devil, Satan. But the name — Lucifer — it means The Bringer of Light: *That* was your name in the Beginning, wasn't it? Well then, Lucifer, *this* is the real you. *This* is the blueprint that the Good Lord had in mind for you."

The subject of the composition was the Entity, and yet it was not. Where the Entity was dark, she had painted Light. Where it was vile, she had painted nobility. Where it was cruel, she had portrayed compassion. Where it was deceitful, she showed the Light of Truth.

The Entity was completely taken aback: It had never expected to be confronted in this way, not least by someone who intended to portray it as something *good!* It did not know what to do: It began to remember, from a far distant past, that once upon a time it *had* been good, it *had* been one of the greatest and noblest and wisest entities that the Lord had ever created, it *had* been a Bringer of Light; and therefore, it was ashamed of what it had become: evil and deceitful and petty and cruel. But in its pride and despair, it would not repent, it became enraged; it would not return to the Good.

And so, the Enemy was not laughing any more: Its face was twisted in torment and fury, it gave out a noise that was a blast, a melding of a deafening roar and a scream. Hope and Angelica and Jesse were blown backward by the blast, off the huge bundle of cables they had been standing on. Slowly, they got up and staggered to their feet, and then all four of them stood and turned and stared in amazement and horror at what was happening now.

The face of the Enemy was contorted and twisted beyond belief in rage and fear; and suddenly it seemed to explode into flame. The four friends held up their hands, shielding their faces from the scorching heat. The Entity then screamed again in its torment, it toppled, and it began falling, falling toward the cold waters of the Bay far below. The four friends ran to the railing of the bridge, and they just caught sight of the blazing being as it crashed into the dark water. The fire was quenched, but the water hissed and boiled into a huge column of steam that billowed up and up, clear up to the low clouds overhead. It drifted away in the howling wind and was gone.

The next morning, Hope, Kimberley and Antoine were relaxing in Monsieur Aubert's studio, drinking their morning coffee and reading the newspaper, when a curious news story caught their eye: The previous evening, according to the article, there had been reports from people who had witnessed strange lights and weird noises, even a shriek and a fireball that had fallen from the Golden Gate Bridge. The article said that the authorities had no difficulty in explaining it away: They stated that it was probable that a bolt of lightning had struck an abandoned vehicle on the Bridge, and that this had caused it to explode in flames and to fall into the Bay. All three friends read the newspaper story together, then they looked at one another, and then they all simply roared with laughter.

"So, is that the end of Lucifer?" Angelica asked Hope. Aubert had gone out. Angelica and Hope had consumed the last of the coffee in his absence and were starting on his wine.

"No, I am afraid not," replied Hope. She thought for a minute, and then said, "No, I should say: I *hope* not. I hope that is not the end of him."

"Why? How could you think that?"

Hope was silent for a while, and then in a quiet voice she said, "Because I have learned to have hope for all of God's creation. Lucifer was not always the Evil One, as we saw him last night. He is part of Creation, one of the noblest spirits, but he has forgotten who he is. He simply gave in to his own pride.

"Angelica, I have never told anyone this before, but there have been many people whom I could not save. There were some who jumped, despite all that I could do. And in every case, it was their pride that kept them locked into their despair. That was why they jumped."

Angelica was silent for a time; and then she said simply, "How horrible!"

"Yes, horrible. And final, it might seem. And yet, Angelica, I do not believe it is final. I learned to pray for those people, those poor, beautiful, desperate people. I learned that even in death, there is hope. I came to believe in a God that is love. I came to believe that God might save them, even if I could not, even though they had condemned themselves. I came to believe that they might be forgiven, even for that pride which led them to their despair."

Angelica thought for a moment, and then she said, "And from what you are saying, I would guess that you believe likewise for that dark Entity whom we saw last night."

"I do, Angelica. It's only pride that keeps him in torment. I pray that one day he will see the light. I pray that he will be forgiven. I pray that he'll be saved."

"So, in a way, you are interceding on his behalf? You would go that far? You would do that for the Prince of Darkness, the evilest, the vilest entity in the Universe?"

"I would. The way I see it, if there's hope for me — and there certainly is, though at one time I had none — then there's hope for everyone, even Lucifer. After all, Angelica, Jesus himself taught us to pray for our enemies. So, then why not pray for the greatest Enemy of all? You see, Angelica, that vile being, that's not the way *I* see him. That's not who he is. *This* is how I see him. *This* is who he is." And Hope held up the sketch she had done, of a Bringer of Light, of Lucifer as he was in the Beginning.

"And Angelica," continued Hope, "there's even more: I believe we are *called* to pray for the evilest, the vilest beings in this fallen world."

Angelica had briefly seen that sketch the evening before, and now in the light of day she was devouring it with her eyes. But she said, "That surely is a compelling idea; I would certainly *want* to believe in it. But surely, you're just being naive, that you're simply believing what you *want* to believe."

Hope smiled a wry smile and replied, "Said like a true cynic. Well, Angelica, in all humility — and in all honesty — I confess that you might be right. But I am willing to put my belief to the test. Besides, how would you want to spend your life? Feeling certain in your cynicism, feeling secure that the physical evidence will back up your ideas? Or would you rather fly free in your faith, and believe without proof?"

"And how will you put it to the test, as you say?" asked Angelica.

"By living in hope," replied Hope.

"And how will you know whether this actually works? Whether or not, say, Lucifer himself is actually saved?"

"You have to understand: The *result* of hoping is not up to me, or you, or anyone but the One. This is not about changing an external Reality, whatever that is. It's about seeing the Reality within and then changing oneself to conform to that Reality.

"How do you mean?"

"It's very simple, really — deceptively simple. It's about living in hope. It's about practicing the art of hope. After all, in the final analysis, what else can one do?"

EPILOGUE

Antoine Aubert continued to work in his studio; and if he had proved a successful artist before, his talent and fame and renown now grew boundlessly. He was never able to match the work of Hope — not in his own mind, anyway — and yet his work rapidly improved, and it expressed a surpassing beauty and insight that approached the divine.

And not long after Angelica's crisis with the Prince of Darkness was over, Monsieur Aubert invited her on a stroll on a beautiful day, and their way took them over the Golden Gate Bridge, and there he knelt and made his proposal to her. She accepted gladly, and soon they were married and settled into a loft that he built above his art studio. They soon after had a daughter: They thought about naming her Hope, after their best friend, but in the end, they decided to name her Faith, which is, after all, the complement to Hope.

And as for Hope, she continued her life in hope, creating beautiful sketches, that the despairing might turn away from Darkness and truly live. She never let her identity become publicly known, lest her left hand come to know what her right was doing; and yet tales and legends sprang up in San Francisco of a woman who saved countless lives — and countless souls. She kept this up until she was very old indeed.

Until finally, one night many years later, Hope's very old friends Antoine and Angelica Aubert had a feeling that they should pay a call on her; and so, they hobbled over to her house. They found her sitting in her chair with a brush in one hand and her palette in the other: She seemed to have fallen asleep with a smile on her face, and she was sitting and facing an enormous canvas. Antoine placed a hand on her shoulder, but Hope didn't move, and then he knew that she had died just as she had lived — composing yet one more uncanny, almost supernatural work.

Antoine was overcome with grief, and he knelt and wept and held Hope's hand; but Angelica's gaze was transfixed on the huge painting, as big as a mural, that Hope had been working on. She perceived its beauty through her tears, and she tapped her husband on the shoulder and exclaimed, "Antoine! Antoine, look at this!"

And old Aubert got up slowly from where he had been kneeling by Hope, and he wiped away his tears, and came and stood by Angelica, and they both gasped in amazement. The painting held the images of all the people Hope had saved or tried to save, hundreds of them, standing on the roadway of the Golden Gate Bridge; and in the foreground, hand in hand, stood her friends Antoine and Angelica. "They are all so beautiful!" they said together. Every one of those souls appeared perfect and surpassingly beautiful, as they were intended in the Beginning. And Aubert, standing there in awe, said in a quiet voice, "*Vraiment*, Hope was the master of hope,"

Antoine and Angelica Aubert passed away soon afterward, but not before Antoine had bequeathed his art studio to Faith, his daughter; and to this day that painting is still displayed in that studio. Hope had left it unsigned, and many are the visitors to that studio who have asked: "Who was the great artist to create such a masterpiece?" In answer, Faith simply shrugs and feigns ignorance, and so the authorship of that extraordinary work remains a mystery.

And secretly, Faith built a tiny chapel within the loft built above her parents' studio; and she knelt within it every day, remembering the faith of her parents, and there she prayed for the salvation of all beings, even of Lucifer. She taught her children to do likewise, and they taught theirs also, generation after generation, never giving up hope. Every one of those prayers has been heard, and perhaps one day those prayers will be granted.

And so, Hope had passed away, and yet she had not. Because you see, to this day, strange tales continue to be told of a woman who suddenly and mysteriously appears to people who are in despair; and she draws sketches of their true selves — images that inspire them to truly live — and she leaves those pictures with them. And those people gaze at their portraits every morning, and they believe that those shining images represent their true selves as they were intended to be. And so, they begin each day studying — and practicing — the Art of Hope.

THE END

www.ingramcontent.com/pod-product-compliance
Lightning Source LLC
Chambersburg PA
CBHW031035190726

48286CB00003BA/1188

9781956691030